First published by Parragon in 2010

Parragon
Queen Street House
4 Queen Street
Bath BA1 1HE, UK

www.chuggington.com

© Ludorum plc 2009

ISBN 978-1-4454-1178-1

Printed in China

CHUGGINGTON

CAN'T CATCH KOKO

Based on the episode "Can't Catch Koko",
written by Di Redmond and Sarah Ball.

PaRRagon

Bath · New York · Singapore · Hong Kong · Cologne · Delhi · Melbourne

One sunny morning, Chuggington's fastest train, Harrison, was in the repair shed. He had broken down the night before and needed a new part.

CLANK!
CLANK!
CLANK!

EXCELLENT

GOOD WORK!

GOOD WORK!

"I need to be fixed fast, Morgan, or I won't be able to make the delivery run tonight," Harrison told the mechanic.

Koko **ZOOMED** excitedly into the fuel yard. She couldn't wait to tell Wilson and Brewster about Harrison. "Who's gonna do the night run if Morgan can't fix him in time?" asked Brewster.

It would have to be someone really fast...
Suddenly, Koko's eyes lit up. She could do it!

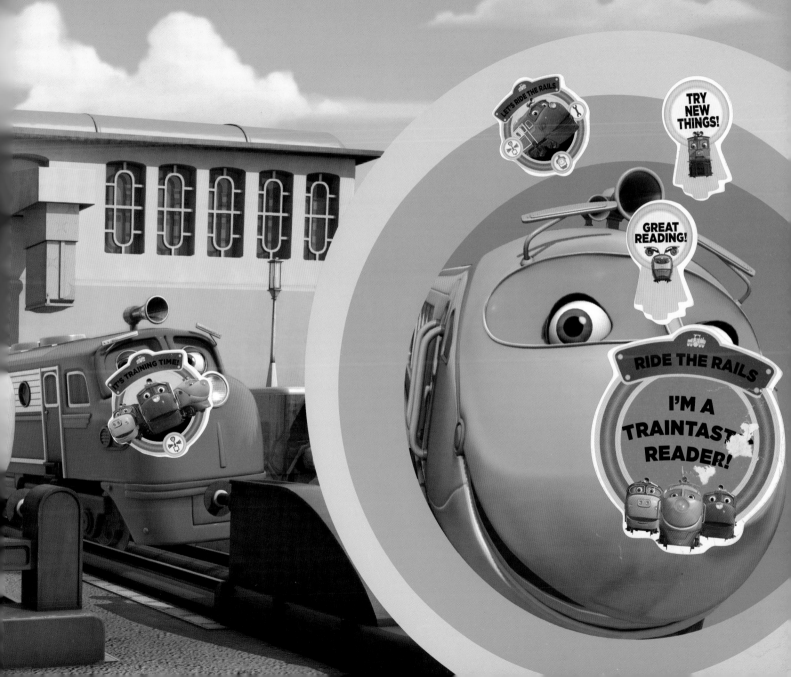

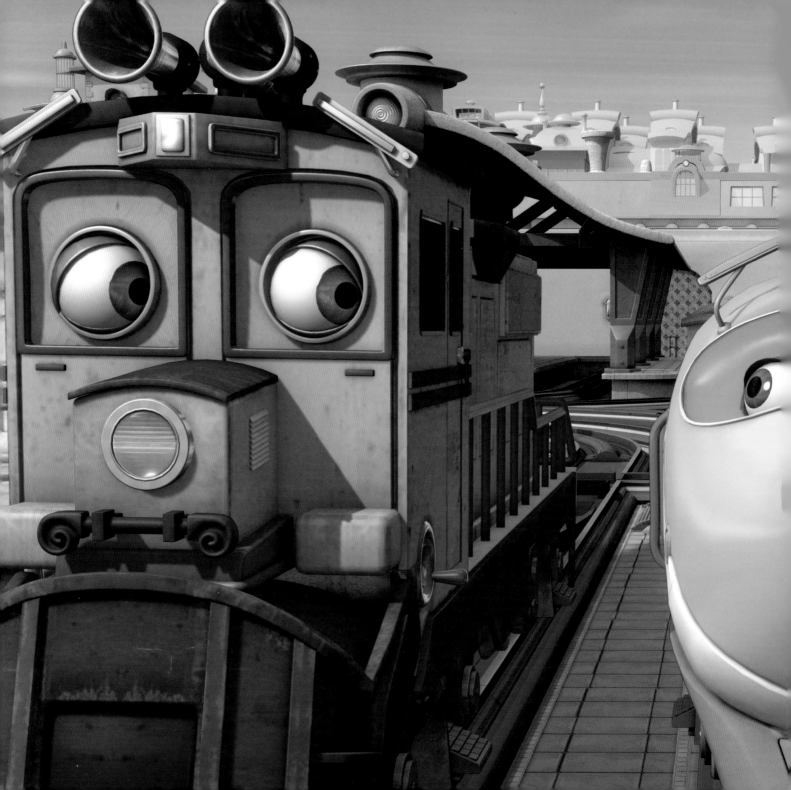

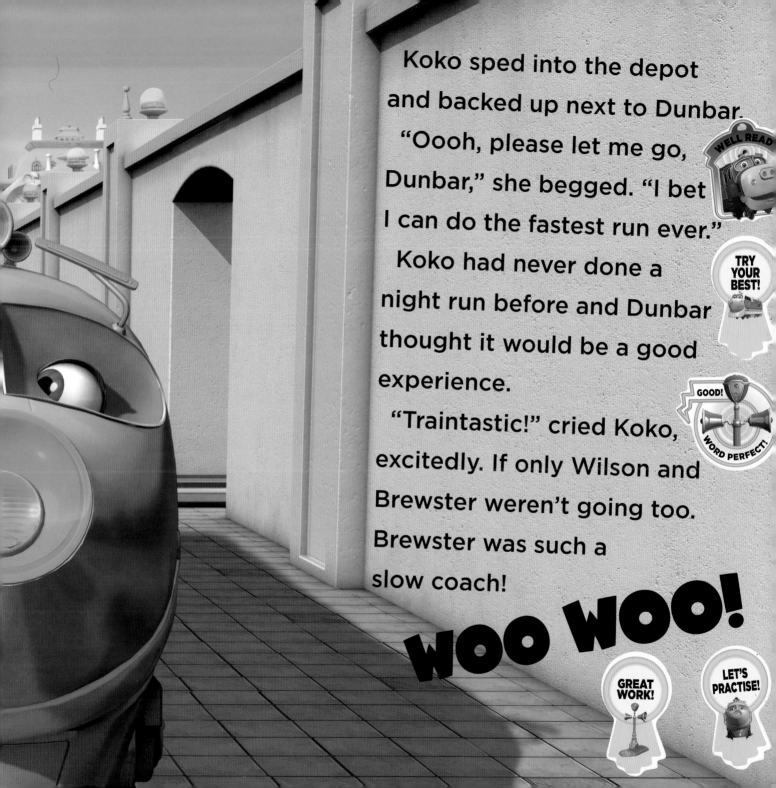

Koko sped into the depot and backed up next to Dunbar. "Oooh, please let me go, Dunbar," she begged. "I bet I can do the fastest run ever." Koko had never done a night run before and Dunbar thought it would be a good experience.

"Traintastic!" cried Koko, excitedly. If only Wilson and Brewster weren't going too. Brewster was such a slow coach!

WOO WOO!

In a flash, the three chuggers were loaded up with goods and were ready to **RIDE THE RAILS**!

At the other end of the tunnel, Wilson and Brewster caught up with Koko. The three friends gasped when they saw the beautiful, moonlit countryside around them.

TWIT-A WOO!

Wilson shuddered at the sound of the owl, but Koko whizzed on ahead.

"Betcha can't catch Koko!" she shouted.

Brewster and Wilson chugged after her. They had to stay together!

TWIT-A WOO!
TWIT-A WOO!

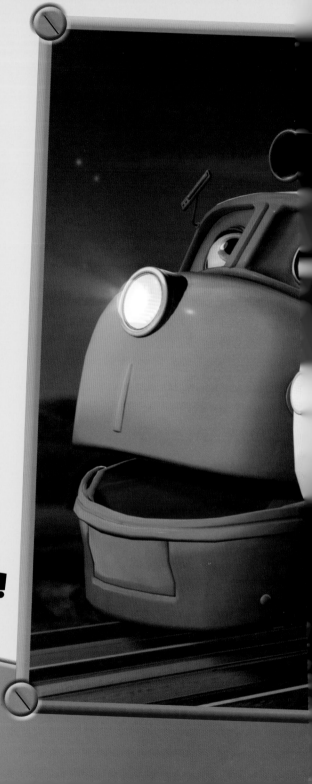

Koko rode down a side track and waited for Wilson and Brewster to appear.

ZOoooooooooo

CHUGGA, CHUGGA! CHOO, CHOO!

Koko could hear their engines getting closer.

A few moments later, Koko jumped out on them.

"BOOOO!"

she yelled, from the hidden track.

"You shouldn't do that Koko, I nearly fell off the track!" Brewster said, crossly.

"If you weren't so slow you would've seen me.

BREWSTER'S A SLOW COACH!"

Koko teased in a sing song voice.

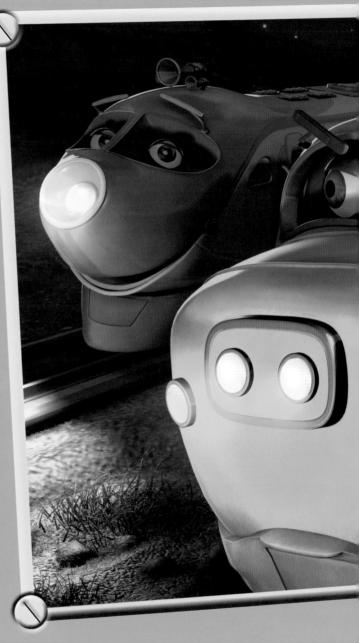

But the chuggers didn't have time to mess around
if they wanted to make the delivery on time. Koko
raced off again, eager to impress Dunbar.

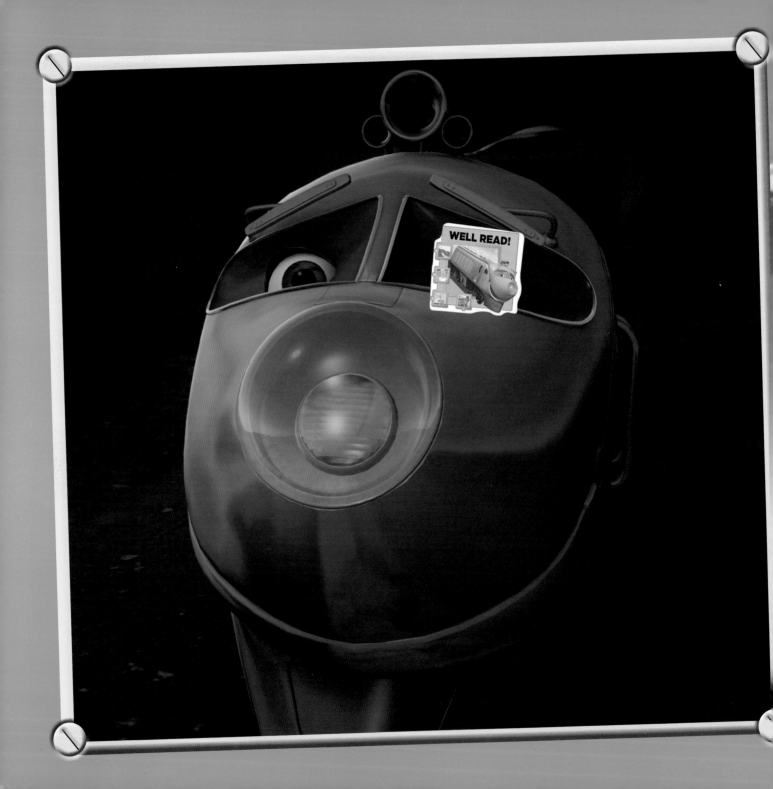

But then...

CREAK, CLUNK, SPLUTTER!

Koko's engine started to make a
funny noise and she stopped moving.

"Wilson? Come back – don't leave
me!" she pleaded.

But her friends had chugged
ahead and were too far
away to hear her.

Wilson and Brewster realised Koko was nowhere in sight. There were no lights on anywhere too – there must have been a power cut.

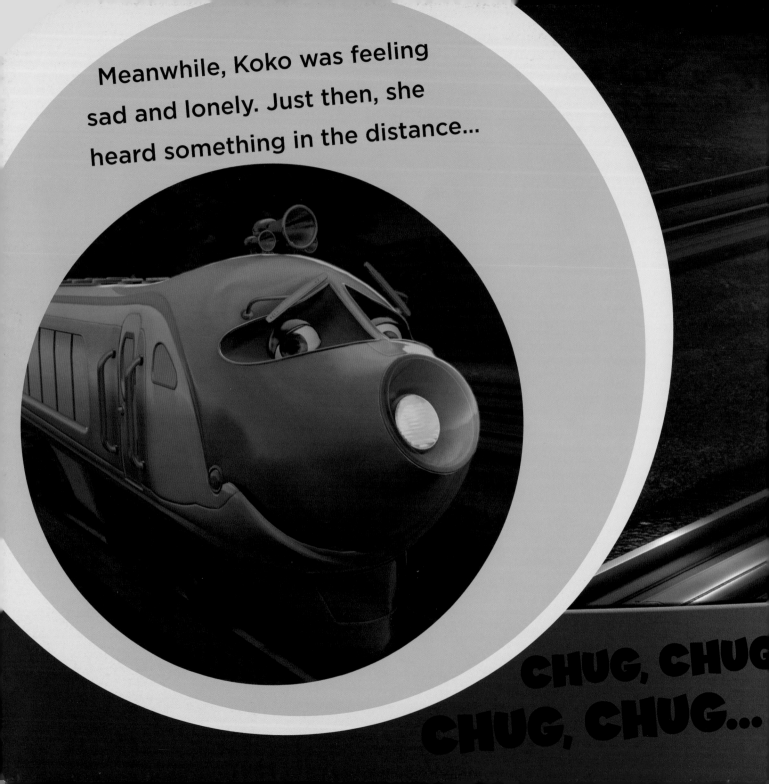

Meanwhile, Koko was feeling sad and lonely. Just then, she heard something in the distance...

CHUG, CHUG, CHUG, CHUG...

It was Wilson and Brewster – they'd come back! Koko learned there was no power in the tracks to charge her engine. Now *she* was the slow coach.

"I'm sorry I teased you, Brewster," she said, quietly.

At the depot, Dunbar was worrying about the trainees.

Wilson suddenly came into sight, towing Koko behind him.

"WOOOOOOO OOOOOOH WOOOOOO OOOOOH!"

cried Wilson, making a loud siren noise.

"Breakdown chugger coming through!"

"Brewster's doing the night run all on his own," Koko told Dunbar.

At last, the power was back and Koko whizzed up and down the track excitedly.

Vee's voice rang out.

I'VE JUST HAD A MESSAGE AND YOU'LL BE PLEASED TO KNOW THAT BREWSTER'S DELIVERED EVERYTHING ON SCHEDULE.

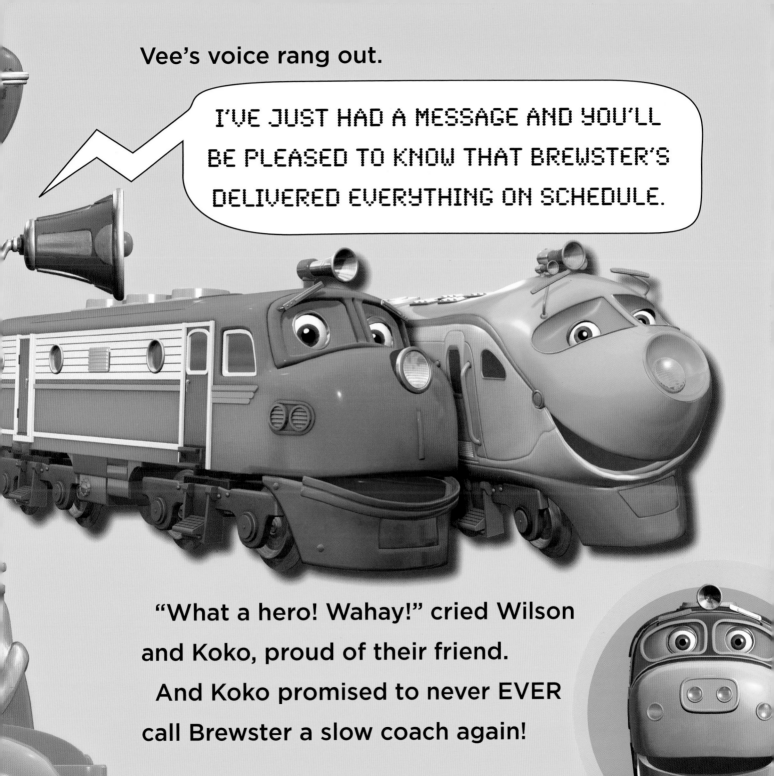

"What a hero! Wahay!" cried Wilson and Koko, proud of their friend.
And Koko promised to never EVER call Brewster a slow coach again!

Complete your Chuggington collection.
Tick them off as you collect!

Stories

1 CLUNKY WILSON — ISBN 978-1-4075-6041-0
2 CAN'T CATCH KOKO — ISBN 978-1-4075-6042-7
3 BRAKING BREWSTER — ISBN 978-1-4075-8009-8
4 WAKE UP WILSON! — ISBN 978-1-4075-8010-4
5 KOKO AND THE TUNNEL — ISBN 978-1-4075-9530-6
6 BREWSTER GOES BANANAS — ISBN 978-1-4075-9531-3

Mini stories

Braking Brewster — ISBN 978-1-4075-9331-9
Clunky Wilson — ISBN 978-1-4075-9332-6
Hodge and the Magnet — ISBN 978-1-4075-9333-3
Koko and the Squirrels — ISBN 978-1-4075-9334-0
Wilson Gets a Wash — ISBN 978-1-4075-9335-7
Zephie's Zoom — ISBN 978-1-4075-9336-4

Activity books

COPY COLOUR POSTER BOOK — ISBN 978-1-4075-6126-4
STICKER SCENE STORY — ISBN 978-1-4075-6044-1
Bumper Sticker Book — ISBN 978-1-4075-8141-5
POSTER BOOK — ISBN 978-1-4075-9529-0
ACTIVITY BOOK — ISBN 978-1-4075-9422-4

Little library

MY FIRST LITTLE LIBRARY — ISBN 978-1-4075-6043-4

Multi-play books

Construct and Play! — ISBN 978-1-4075-9882-6
— ISBN 978-1-4075-9884-0

Annual

CHUGGINGTON ANNUAL 2011 — ISBN 978-1-84535-437-4

Activity pack

CHUGGER TRAVEL PACK — ISBN 978-1-4075-9885-7

3D books

3D — ISBN 978-1-4075-8349-5
Chugger Sticker Colouring Pad — ISBN 978-1-4075-9780-5

Play books

— ISBN 978-1-4075-6127-1
KOKO ON CALL — ISBN 978-1-4075-8142-2

Story collection

Storybook Collection — ISBN 978-1-4075-6046-5

Train books

WILSON — ISBN 978-1-4075-8138-5
KOKO — ISBN 978-1-4075-8139-2
BREWSTER — ISBN 978-1-4075-8140-8

GOOD
EFFORT!